THE UNTIDY LITTLE HEDGEHOG

BY

MOLLY BRETT

© The Medici Society Ltd., London 1966. Printed in England. Ref. 563

2

Fuzzy, the untidy little hedgehog, lived very comfortably with Miss Mole, until the day when she ran across the field to buy a pennyworth of bee's wax from Mr. Bumble Bee.

Miss Mole was a neat and tidy little creature, and intended to polish her set of chestnut furniture with the bee's wax.

On the way back she tripped over a magnifying glass which had dropped out of somebody's pocket, for she was very shortsighted.

Miss Mole picked it up wondering what it could be; then she noticed a strange thing—the leaves and berries nearby seemed bigger and brighter when she looked at them through it.

This was a wonderful find and she hurried home, peering through the glass as she went, delighted to see everything so clearly.

But there was a shock for Miss Mole when she inspected her house through the magnifying glass; it was not nice and clean as she expected, for there were fingermarks, and even scribbles, on the walls, the door handles looked sticky, and, as for the floor—well— when seen through the glass it was clear that SOMEONE had not wiped their feet on the doormat.

3

Miss Mole followed the muddy footprints to the little hedgehog's room.

It was very untidy indeed and so was he; his prickles were not brushed and his paws were not washed.

"You *horrid* little hedgehog!" scolded Miss Mole, "your finger marks are all over the walls, your prickles need combing, your paws want a wash, and— you have *never* wiped your feet, so—
OUT YOU GO!"
and she chased him through the door.

Fuzzy ran away from the angry mole across the fields, and right in front of a big farm tractor clattering home over the hill.

Thinking some strange monster was after him he scrambled through the hedge into a lane beyond, then under the gate leading to a cottage where he came to a window and peeped inside.

The room within was lighted by a cheerful fire, before it a small dog and a large cat lay fast asleep.

The window was not properly fastened so Fuzzy crept in quietly and curled up beside them.

4

But—HE FORGOT HIS PRICKLES and—next moment—

"PINS!" barked the little dog, "Bow! Wow! Wow!"
and

"NEEDLES!" mewed the large cat, "Miaow! Miaow! Miaow!"

In came their mistress to see what the noise was about.

She seized the tongs, picked up Fuzzy, popped him in the dustbin, and banged down the lid.

Presently he heard a rustle and a little mouse popped out from the wastepaper and empty tins.

"We *must* escape when the lid is lifted," she squeaked, "before the great DUST VAN DRAGON comes, for he is fed on all the rubbish and will swallow us too!"

Early next morning they were wakened by a loud roaring and

rumbling—the DUST VAN DRAGON had arrived!

Big boots approached the dustbin, the lid was taken off, and the dustman carried the bin away.

In a moment the mouse and hedgehog scrambled out and leapt wildly into space.

As they did so Fuzzy caught a glimpse of an enormous machine, with great black mouth wide open, the Dust Van Dragon itself waiting for breakfast.

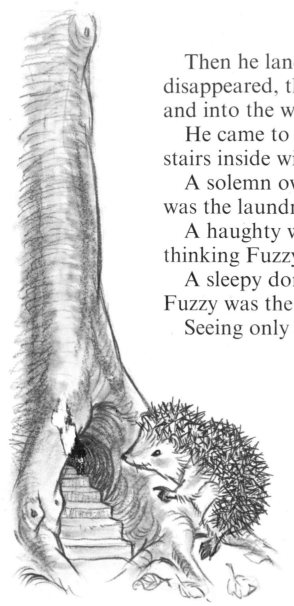

Then he landed with a bump, and, as the mouse had disappeared, the little hedgehog scuttled off down the lane and into the wood.

He came to a big tree with a hole in the trunk. There were stairs inside with little doors opening on to them.

A solemn owl peered out of the first door, thinking Fuzzy was the laundry coming up.

A haughty woodpecker looked out of the second door thinking Fuzzy was the baker.

A sleepy dormouse looked out of the third door, thinking Fuzzy was the postman.

Seeing only a little hedgehog they slammed their doors, and he went on up the stairs where another door flew open, and a squirrel rushed out and pulled him inside.

"The Baby Sitter at last!" she chattered, "Here are my children, Conker and Hazel, brush their tails and then take them for a walk, while I go over to Beech Wood to find some nuts."

Then she skipped away before Fuzzy could explain that he was *not* the baby sitter.

9

So the little hedgehog started to brush the squirrels' tails; they looked rather odd because he was not very handy with a hairbrush.

"*Now* we'll go for a walk to meet Mummy," squeaked Hazel and Conker, and ran *upstairs* to the very top of the tree, out through a hole, and along a branch.

A walk in the *treetops*! the little hedgehog had not expected *that,* but he started off after the squirrels along a branch, which swayed in the wind and bent under his weight.

Fuzzy wobbled and wobbled, then lost his balance, went tumbling down through twigs and boughs, and finally bounced safely on a carpet of dead leaves far below.

He picked himself up and skipped along gaily, splashing through the puddles, and kicking up the fallen leaves as he went.

Then he sat on all the toadstools he could see until they broke under his weight, and when a passing pigeon told him to stop he threw acorns at her.

After that Fuzzy found a fir cone and kicked it along like a football until it landed on Mrs. Toad's little stall of jellied worms.

13

The animals who lived in the wood were very cross.

"What a *naughty* little hedgehog!" they grumbled, and called all the birds, who swooped down and a disapproving magpie dropped him in a litter bin.

Fuzzy curled into a prickly ball until the coast was clear, then he climbed out, upsetting the bin and scattering the contents everywhere.

It took the birds a long time to put it all back after the untidy little hedgehog had disappeared under a fence, and into a garden where there was a large rubbish heap in a corner, and, sitting on top of it was the mouse.

"I was on the lookout for you," she squeaked, and invited him to stay with all her family.

They danced round singing in squeaky voices,

"Fuzzy shall be king of the castle,"

before leading him inside where they had made long passages, and cosy little rooms.

It was just the home for him, being dreadfully untidy, as dead leaves, sticks, and the garden rubbish were always being added to it.

One day a robin called with the latest news.

"The children in the house are having a party this evening, and there is a big box of groceries waiting in the porch."

"Do you think there might be any *cheese* in it?" asked Mrs. Mouse.

Fuzzy knew that she loved cheese so he offered to go and see.

It was a dull November day and getting dark quickly, but there was the box of groceries in the porch.

Fuzzy peeped inside; what queer groceries they were! Certainly not cheese but could they be sausages?

Just then the door opened and some children and a man came out.

"Fireworks first," he said, picking up the box, "and then we'll set light to the rubbish heap and have A FINE BONFIRE."

A few minutes later there was a loud BANG! and a shower of coloured lights.

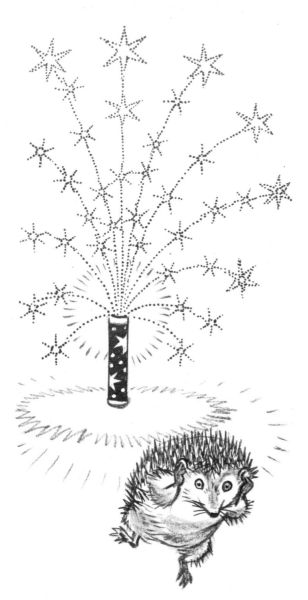

Fuzzy's prickles stood on end with fright, but the mice *must* be warned that their home was to be a bonfire, so he started off down the garden as fast as he could go.

It was a terrifying journey, and often he stopped to hide as the fireworks popped and banged, with falling stars, the WHOOSH! of rockets, and weird lights flashing red, green, and blue.

But at last the little hedgehog scrambled into the mouse's home.

Breathless and scared he panted, "The FIREWORKS are coming, our rubbish heap is going to be a BONFIRE! Run away and hide as fast as you can."

And off ran the mice as they heard voices and footsteps coming along the garden path.

The children crowded round the rubbish heap, a match flickered, then flames shot up and the last fireworks popped and sparkled.

19

When at last the fire died down and the excitement was over the children went back to the house.

Early next morning Fuzzy and the mice found only a circle of blackened sticks, and a smell of wood smoke.

As the sun rose through the autumn mist the mice

started to dig a new hole in the nearby bank between the roots of an old tree, where they would be safe and warm during the winter.

But hedgehogs cannot fit into mouse holes so Fuzzy had to look for a new home.

He asked if he might stay in the rabbits' burrow, or the guineapigs' hutch, but was told he was *much* too prickly.

Sadly Fuzzy wandered away until he came to a doll's pram—would it make a house for him?

He climbed into it and came face to face with—a great big BEAR.

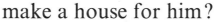

The little hedgehog did not know it was only a toy Teddy, and he fell out of the pram in a fright, curled into a tight ball.

Then he started to roll down a slope and he could not stop, bumped down two stone steps and—SPLASH! into a lily pool.

Two frogs helped him out spluttering and dripping.

"Put in the dustbin, nearly burnt on the bonfire, nobody wants me with all these prickles, no home for the winter, and now I'm wet through," sobbed poor Fuzzy.

The garden robin flew down to comfort him.

"See how nice and clean you look after your bath," he chirped, helping the hedgehog to dry himself with a leaf.

"And I found just the thing to keep your prickles tidy," he added,

producing a small comb, which he had hidden under a fern.

Soon Fuzzy looked the very neatest of little hedgehogs, and was just admiring his reflection in the pool when a little boy saw him, tied him up in his handkerchief, and ran to ask his mother if he could keep him as a pet.

But the answer was "No, hedgehogs are so prickly, and grubby too."

"Oh Mummy, this is such a neat tidy little hedgehog," pleaded the child, tipping Fuzzy out of the handkerchief.

When she saw his clean face and paws, his soft fur waistcoat, and carefully combed prickles, the mother said he might live in the tool shed, in a cosy box full of hay, with a saucer of milk beside it.

So Fuzzy has found a home at last, and his new friend helps him to

keep tidy by brushing his prickles every day.

He is always careful to wipe his feet, and sometimes friends come to tea, but any young hedgehog turning up with dirty paws and tangled prickles is led off to robin and his little comb, because Fuzzy is now quite sure that nobody likes you much if you are always UNTIDY.